OTTO Goes to the Beach

Todd PARR

Megan Tingley Books
LITTLE, BROWN AND COMPANY
New York An AOL Time Warner Company

To Liz, Gerry, Luigi, and Pienza
Love, Todd

Also by Todd Parr

The Best Friends Book
Big & Little
Black & White
The Daddy Book
Do's and Don'ts
The Feel Good Book
The Feelings Book
Funny Faces
Going Places
It's Okay to Be Different
The Mommy Book
My Really Cool Baby Book
The Okay Book
Things That Make You Feel Good / Things That Make You Feel Bad
This Is My Hair
Underwear Do's and Don'ts
Zoo Do's and Don'ts

First Edition

Library of Congress Cataloging-in-Publication Data
Parr, Todd.
Otto goes to the beach / Todd Parr.—1st ed.
p. cm.
Summary: When Otto the dog feels lonely, he drives to the beach hoping to find a friend to play with.
ISBN 0-316-73870-0
[1. Dogs—Fiction. 2. Friendship—Fiction. 3. Beaches—Fiction. 4. Animals—Fiction.] I. Title.
PZ7.P2447 Ot 2003
[E]—dc21 2002072986

10 9 8 7 6 5 4 3 2 1

TWP

Printed in Singapore

This is Otto.
"Woof, woof!"

He doesn't like to be
left home alone.

Poor Otto!

One day he decides to go find someone to play with. He gets into the car and drives to the beach.

Otto sits in his favorite
chair and puts on sunscreen.
I hope I meet a friend
here, he thinks.

SPF 100

Otto sees a crab and asks, "Do you want to build a sand castle with me?" But the crab says, "I'm too crabby!" So Otto has to do it by himself.

Poor Otto!

It is hot. Otto decides to get in the water to cool off. He sees a lot of fish and tries to swim with them, but they all swim the other way.

Poor Otto!

Soon Otto is hungry. He goes to the snack bar for a treat. "Do you have any bones?" he asks. But they only have ice cream, and it melts all over his nose.

Poor Otto!

SNACK BAR

Otto goes surfing with a cat. It is fun, but then a big wave comes and his bathing suit falls off and the cat laughs at him.

Poor Otto!

HA HA

Otto is sad. Nobody likes
to do the same things
he likes to do. He decides
to take a nap.

Suddenly a loud noise wakes him up. It is another dog. She is digging up bones in the sand.

"That's my favorite game!" says Otto.

"Mine too!" says the dog. "Do you want to play with me?"

So Otto and his new friend play together the rest of the day. And Otto isn't lonely anymore.

LUCKY OTTO!

Sometimes it's hard to make new friends, but remember, there is always someone out there who will like to play with you.

Love,

OTTO and Todd